To Tracy, for being my Muse and Inspiration.
To Doreen Lee, the first and best editor I ever had.
And to Fosco El Doggo, for keeping me sane.

T. L.

To the memory of my mother,
Daniela; to my light, Ariane; and
to the next generation of pirate
women, Kaya and Lara

S. H.

Text copyright © 2019 by Tony Lee
Illustrations copyright © 2019 by Sam Hart

Colored by Tarsis Cruz with Flavio Costa
Lettered by Cadu Simões

First U.S. edition 2019

Library of Congress Catalog Card Number 2018961812
ISBN 978-1-5362-0019-5

APS 24 23 22 21 20 19
10 9 8 7 6 5 4 3 2 1

Printed in Humen, Dongguan, China

This book was typeset in CCWildWords.
The illustrations were created digitally.

Candlewick Press
99 Dover Street
Somerville, Massachusetts 02144

visit us at www.candlewick.com

Pirate Queen

THE LEGEND OF GRACE O'MALLEY

Pirate Queen

THE LEGEND OF GRACE O'MALLEY

WRITTEN BY
TONY LEE

ILLUSTRATED BY
SAM HART

COLORED BY
TARSIS CRUZ WITH **FLAVIO COSTA**

LETTERED BY
CADU SIMÕES

CANDLEWICK PRESS

The Irish Rebellion against Henry VIII led by Silken Thomas, the Earl of Kildare, has failed, and the leaders have been executed.

Henry VIII is now the uncontested king of Ireland — the lords of Ireland are now expected to surrender their lands to the throne in the hope that those lands will be returned in exchange for their loyalty.

Many never see their lands again.

The Irish are forced to follow the English Tudor rule, under which their churches are ransacked, their language ignored, their people oppressed. English lords are given Irish lands, and Irish clans find that their claims of succession fall on deaf ears.

But there is a storm coming.

In Connacht, Ireland, the chieftain Eoghan Dubhdara Ó Máille, known in legend as Dubhdara O'Malley, has a daughter named Gráinne Ní Mháille — better known as Gráinne Mhaol, or Granuaile. And this girl will one day bring the fight to the English, become a thorn in the side of Queen Elizabeth herself, and become a legend in the process.

For there is indeed a storm coming — and her name is Grace O'Malley, the Pirate Queen of Ireland. . . .

I NEED TO LEAVE TOMORROW FOR *SPAIN* — WE NEED TO PREPARE FOR THE SUMMER TRADING.

TAKE ME WITH YOU, DA'! TEACH ME THE WAYS OF THE SEA!

YOU'RE FIFTEEN, GRACE. YOU'RE ALMOST A WOMAN.

YOU NEED TO BE LEARNING A WOMAN'S SKILLS. NOT SAILING AROUND THE WORLD.

A WOMAN'S SKILLS? *NEEDLEWORK AND DANCING?*

I'M AN O'MALLEY! WE DON'T DANCE!

YES, YOU'RE AN O'MALLEY. YOU BRING THE STORMS AND LAUGH FIRE.

BUT UNLESS WE TURN ENEMIES TO ALLIES, THE ENGLISH WILL TAKE *EVERYTHING* WE'VE BUILT OVER THE YEARS.

COME, GRACE, WE NEED TO RETURN TO THE KEEP... THE *O'FLAHERTY CLAN* WILL HAVE ARRIVED BY NOW.

THE O'FLAHERTYS? I *HATE* THEM!

THEIR SON'S A FOOL!

THE GREAT HALL OF THE O'MALLEYS.

DUBHDARA! YOU HAVEN'T AGED A DAY!

AND YOU LIE LIKE AN ENGLISHMAN, GILLEY!

SO, HAVE YOU THOUGHT OVER OUR OFFER?

I HAVE, AND IT'S A MIGHTY TEMPTING ONE.

I NEED TO THINK ABOUT IT STILL—BUT YOU SHALL HAVE MY *ANSWER* WHEN I RETURN FROM SPAIN.

HOW GOES IT TO THE SOUTH?

THE ENGLISH POKE AT US, BUT WE POKE BACK HARDER.

AFTER ALL, *FORTUNE FAVOURS THE BRAVE!*

LIVING YOUR LIVES BASED ON A MOTTO ISN'T THE BEST WAY...

CLANG!

WHAT'S THAT NOISE? IT SOUNDS LIKE *FIGHTING!*

IF YOU'VE *DOUBLE-CROSSED* US, GILLEY—

I SWEAR! I KNOW NOTHING ABOUT THIS.

TAKE IT BACK, DONAL! TAKE BACK WHAT YOU SAID!

CLANG!

NO! I STAND BY MY WORDS!

NOW PUT DOWN THE SWORD AND FETCH ME SOME FOOD, WENCH!

I HATE YOU! YOU'RE A FOOL!

LIKE I CARE WHAT A GIRL THINKS!

SWISH!

WHAT IS THIS? STOP THIS RIGHT NOW!

HE STARTED IT! HE TOLD ME I LOOKED PRETTY IN A DRESS, LIKE I'M NOTHING BUT A VAIN LITTLE GIRL!

HE ALWAYS MOCKS ME FOR BEING A GIRL! I'M AS GOOD AS HE IS AT EVERYTHING!

I HATE HIM! MAKE HIM LEAVE!

I CAN'T DO THAT, GRACE. I'M SORRY...

...BUT THE O'FLAHERTY CLAN WILL BE FOSTERING YOU WHILE I'M GONE.

NO...

THAT NIGHT.

HEY! YOU! WHERE DO YOU THINK YOU'RE —

GRACE?

I'M SORRY, DONAL, BUT I'M GOING WITH MY DA' TO SPAIN. I DON'T WANT TO STAY HERE.

DOES HE KNOW?

SPAIN.

TAKE CARE OF THE SHIP WHILE I'M GONE! THIS WON'T TAKE LONG!

WHAT'S THE MATTER?

THOSE TRADERS — THEY SEEMED MIGHTY INTERESTED IN WHO BLACK OAK *WAS*, RATHER THAN WHAT HE WANTED TO *TRADE*.

I THINK THEY'RE WORKING FOR THE *ENGLISH*. HENRY HAS SPIES EVERYWHERE.

OF COURSE, THIS COULD JUST BE THE WORRIES OF A CYNICAL —

GRACE? WHERE DID SHE GO?

GRACE!

AND WE HAVE MUCH SPICE TO SEND BACK TO ENGLAND.

I DON'T TRADE WITH ENGLAND.

AH YES, I FORGOT THAT—

DA'!!! LOOK OUT!!

HNF!

LEAVE HIM! WE'RE EXPOSED!

THAT'S IT! RUN BACK TO HENRY!

TELL HIM THE O'MALLEYS CAN'T BE KILLED!

GRACE! WHAT ARE YOU DOING HERE? AND WHAT HAPPENED TO YOUR HAIR?

I CUT IT SO I COULD STOW AWAY ON BOARD YOUR SHIP!

I'M SORRY, DA', BUT I KNEW SOMETHING BAD WAS GONNA HAPPEN! I HAD TO DO IT!

FINN KNEW ABOUT THIS, DIDN'T HE? I'LL BE HAVING WORDS WITH HIM WHEN I GET BACK.

WHO GAVE YOU THE SWORD?

DONAL. HE SAW ME LEAVING.

LOOKS LIKE I'LL BE HAVING WORDS WITH A LOT OF PEOPLE.

A YEAR PASSES...

10 SEPTEMBER 1547.

WHAT IS IT?

LOOKS LIKE A *BATTLE* OFF THE COAST OF SCOTLAND.

THE EARL OF HUNTLEY'S A FRIEND. WE SHOULD CHECK IN, MAKE SURE HE'S ALL RIGHT.

THOSE ARE *ENGLISH* FLAGS! IS IT KING HENRY?

NO, WE HEARD HE'D DIED. THIS WILL BE THE NEW RULER.

RAISE SAILS! WE'RE MOVING IN — BUT BE READY TO LEAVE IN A HURRY!

SIRE! A SHIP DOCKS BELOW!

WHO? ENGLISH? *SHOW ME!*

BLACK OAK O'MALLEY. OH, THE GODS ARE KIND TO ME TODAY.

WE MIGHT STILL GET THE *CHILD* TO SAFETY.

LORD SOMERSET'S MEN ARE WINNING, O'MALLEY.

BUT WE'LL DIE TO A MAN IF IT MEANS THAT SHE CAN ESCAPE.

WHO CAN ESCAPE?

MARY, QUEEN OF SCOTLAND.

YOU CAN'T BE *SERIOUS*! THAT CHILD IS NO OLDER THAN FOUR, FIVE YEARS OF AGE!

AND SHE BECAME QUEEN WHEN SHE WAS *SIX DAYS OLD*.

BEFORE HENRY DIED, HE WANTED HER TO MARRY HIS SON, AND THE ENGLISH STILL WANT THE ALLIANCE.

THEY STILL WANT TO RULE SCOTLAND!

I'M NOT A FREEDOM FIGHTER! I'M A SAILOR!

THE *HELL* YOU ARE! YOU'RE LEADER OF THE O'MALLEY CLAN, AND YOU HATE THE ENGLISH AS MUCH AS WE DO!

ALL WE NEED IS MARY TAKEN SOMEWHERE *SAFE* — A PRIORY NEAR STIRLING. PEOPLE WILL MEET YOU BY THE RIVERBANK.

ALL RIGHT, BUT ONLY BECAUSE I HAVE A DAUGHTER.

I'LL TAKE YOUR QUEEN TO STIRLING.

CONNACHT — HOME OF DONAL AND GRACE.

LORD DONAL! YOU *DON'T* WANT TO GO IN THERE TODAY!

THE LADY'S IN A FOUL MOOD!

WHAT'S SHE DOING NOW? CAN A MAN GET NO REST?

I'M SICK OF NEEDLEWORK AND WEARING DRESSES! YOU CAN'T MAKE ME, DONAL O'FLAHERTY!

I'M YOUR *HUSBAND*, GRACE! AND YOU'RE A CHIEFTAIN'S WIFE! YOU NEED TO *ACT* LIKE ONE! NO MORE BATTLES! NO MORE FIGHTS! STOP *PIRATING* THE ENGLISH SHIPS AND LOOK AFTER OUR CHILDREN!

THAT'S ALL I DO! GIVE YOU BABIES AND LOOK AFTER THEM!

OWEN! MARGARET! MURROUGH! DO YOU EVEN REMEMBER THEIR NAMES?

OF COURSE I DO! I CAN'T HELP THE FACT THAT I'M *CHIEFTAIN!* I GET BACK WHEN I CAN!

THE ENGLISH ARE AT OUR DOOR — WE HAVE TO FIGHT!

I KNOW. IT'S JUST...

...I'M NOT THIS WOMAN, NO MATTER WHAT YOU WANT. I'M A SAILOR, NOT A MOTHER.

I KNOW, GRACE. BUT THE CHILDREN NEED YOU. AND MY *PEOPLE* NEED A LADY WHEN THE LORD IS AWAY.

WEAR WHAT YOU WANT. I DON'T CARE...

AND TO THINK YOU SAID YOU LOVED ME. *LIAR.*

KNEW IT THE DAY I GAVE YOU MY SWORD.

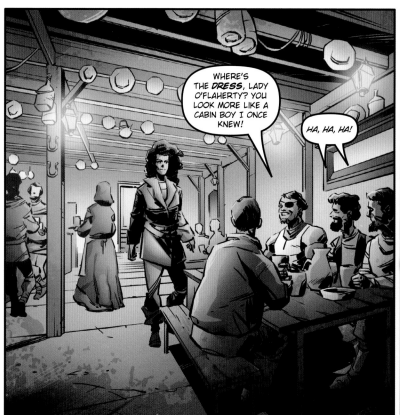

WHERE'S THE **DRESS**, LADY O'FLAHERTY? YOU LOOK MORE LIKE A CABIN BOY I ONCE KNEW!

HA, HA, HA!

EVEN WEARING MY DRESS, I COULD STILL **OUTDRINK** YOU, ONE-EYE McCORMICK!

TO FINN, AND ALL THE OTHERS WHO DIED PROTECTING US FROM...

...INVADERS.

AYE!

GRACE O'FLAHERTY! WHY DO YOU STAY IN THE TOWER MAKING DRESSES? COME BACK TO THE HIGH SEAS AND PIRATE THE ENGLISH!

DONAL WON'T EMPLOY ME BECAUSE OF MY EYE, SO COME WITH US AND BE DAMNED!

GRACE O'FLAHERTY IS A **LADY** AND IS SHOCKED BY YOUR TONE, ONE-EYE! SHE WOULD NEVER LEAVE HER HUSBAND!

BUT **GRACE O'MALLEY** IS MADE FROM STERNER STUFF.

SHE SAYS YOU'RE ALWAYS WELCOME IN CONNACHT. AND ONE DAY SHE MIGHT TAKE YOU UP ON THAT OFFER.

BUNOWEN CASTLE, CONNACHT.

THAT'S RIGHT, OWEN! KEEP YOUR GUARD UP!

YOU TEACH YOUR BOYS SO WELL, GRACE. BUT WON'T DONAL BE ANNOYED WHEN HE RETURNS?

I LOVE MY HUSBAND DEARLY— BUT HE ALSO KNOWS THAT I'M A *BETTER FIGHTER* THAN HE IS! I CAN FIGHT WITH BOTH HANDS, FOR A START!

HAS IT REALLY BEEN *TEN YEARS*? I USED TO HATE HIM. UNTIL HE GAVE ME HIS LOVE. AND A SWORD.

NOW I WAIT FOR HIM TO RETURN FROM WHATEVER *FIGHT* HE'S BEEN IN. MY PIRATING DAYS ARE OVER.

YES, YOU WAIT PATIENTLY AT HOME, DON'T YOU, MA'AM?

NOT ONCE HAVE YOU SNEAKED OUT AND *PLUNDERED WITH PIRATES!*

IF DONAL'S GOING TO LEAVE SOLDIERS AND SAILORS HERE, HE HAS TO ACCEPT THEY'RE UNDER *MY CONTROL!*

AND AS SUCH, THEY MIGHT HAVE TO LET ME SAIL WITH THEM NOW AND THEN.

LADY O'FLAHERTY! I BRING TERRIBLE NEWS FROM *LOUGH CORRIB!*

THAT'S... THAT'S WHERE DONAL WENT! WHAT IS IT?

I'M AFRAID DONAL O'FLAHERTY HAS BEEN KILLED BY THE JOYCES!

BUNOWEN CASTLE, CONNACHT.

WE'RE ALL PACKED, MA'AM.

ARE YOU SURE YOU WANT TO LEAVE?

THERE'S NOTHING BUT *MEMORIES* HERE FOR ME NOW.

I'M NOT THE CHIEFTAIN, AND MY CHILDREN ARE TOO YOUNG TO CHALLENGE THE ENGLISH. WE MUST GO BACK TO SAFER GROUND.

THE ENGLISH WANT ME *DEAD*. THEY'LL COME HERE SOON. SO I HAVE TO LEAVE.

YOU'RE WELCOME TO COME WITH ME, BACK TO CLARE ISLAND, BUT IT'S O'MALLEY LAND.

IF YOU WISH TO LEAVE, HOWEVER, THEN DEPART AS FAMILY.

WE'LL BE LEAVING YOU TONIGHT, LADY GRACE. I NEVER FOUND MY SEA LEGS.

THE LIFE OF A PIRATE WAS NEVER FOR ME.

WE HEAR THAT *RICHARD BURKE* IS RAISING AN ARMY AGAINST THE ENGLISH. I RECKON THAT'S WHERE WE'LL GO.

SOME OF THE JOYCES ARE COMING WITH US. WE'D WELCOME YOU TOO, IF YOU EVER CHANGE YOUR MIND.

RICHARD OF THE IRONS? I KNOW HIM. A GOOD MAN, EVEN IF HE'S A SCOUNDREL.

TELL HIM TO TREAT YOU WELL, OR HE'LL HAVE THE *PIRATE QUEEN* TO ANSWER TO.

SAFE JOURNEY, O'FLAHERTYS AND JOYCES.

MAY YOUR SHIP SAIL STRAIGHT, GRACE O'MALLEY.

YOU CAN HAVE ME, BUT LEAVE GRACE OUT OF THIS! SHE'S FOUND PEACE!

COME ON, O'MALLEY! SHE *STILL* PIRATES THE SEA!

BESIDES, THE ORDER HAS ALREADY BEEN SENT. OUR ALLY HAS PAID US WELL FOR IT. YOU MAY KNOW HIM.

AYE. BLOODY BINGHAM, ISN'T IT? HE'S BEEN A POX ON MY FAMILY SINCE WE SAVED QUEEN MARY.

LOOKS LIKE I HAVE NO OPTION, THEN...

O'MALL—

CHLINK CHLINK CHLINK

SHAME. HE USED TO BE A GOOD MAN. STILL, GOLD IS GOLD.

PASS ME A DAGGER, WILL YOU? BINGHAM WANTED A *MESSAGE* SENT TO THE IRISH.

THE BIG DOG IS DEAD...

... NOW IT'S TIME TO PUT DOWN THE *RABID PUP.*

WILL YOU GET *OUT* OF HERE, PADRAIG MacMAHON! I KNOW WHAT TO DO!

JUST MAKE HER WEAR THE *CLOAK*, OISIN! BRIGHT RED AGAINST SNOW MAKES AN IDEAL TARGET!

OISIN, KEEP DINNER HOT FOR US. WE'RE GOING FOR A RIDE.

THE SNOW MAKES THE LAND LOOK QUITE BEAUTIFUL.

OF COURSE, MA'AM. AND PLEASE, PUT YOUR CLOAK ON. IT'S *BITTERLY COLD* OUT THERE!

REALLY? THAT BRIGHT THING? I'LL SCARE OFF ALL THE ANIMALS!

I HEAR THAT RED IS HUGH DE LACY'S FAVOURITE COLOUR...

OH, I *SEE* NOW! GIVE ME THAT, THEN!

I'LL BE BACK FOR DINNER!

SLAM

NO, YOU WON'T.

ROCKFLEET CASTLE — HOME OF RICHARD BURKE.

I'M SORRY TO HEAR OF YOUR FATHER'S DEATH, GRACE. I KNOW YOU TOOK REVENGE ON THE MacMAHONS...

...BUT THE *REAL* KILLERS WILL BE BROUGHT TO JUSTICE.

THE *REAL* KILLERS ARE IN *ENGLAND*, RICHARD, SO I'LL HAVE TO DO WITH KILLING ALL THE ENGLISH I CAN FIND.

I'M NO *SOLDIER*, THOUGH. I PROPOSE A JOINT AGREEMENT.

A *MARRIAGE*. A YEAR AND A DAY. I GAIN ROCKFLEET CASTLE, AND YOU GAIN THE *O'MALLEY FLEET*.

BETWEEN US WE CAN SECURE WESTERN IRELAND FROM THE ENGLISH. MY PEOPLE WILL BE SAFE.

I GET YOUR FLEET *AND* YOUR HAND IN MARRIAGE? WHAT FOOL WOULD TURN THAT DOWN?

DONE! WE WED LATER TODAY!

YOU'LL TAKE THE *BURKE* NAME, OF COURSE.

OVER MY DEAD BODY, HUSBAND.

DAMN THAT WOMAN! WHY WON'T SHE DIE?

YOU HAVE TO GIVE HER CREDIT. SHE'S DONE WONDERFULLY SINCE YOU TRIED TO KILL HER. THE *FIRST* TIME, THAT IS.

AND NOW SHE KNOWS YOU KILLED HER FATHER...

IT WAS SUPPOSED TO *BREAK HER*! NOT *INSPIRE HER*!

AND NOW SHE'S ALLIED WITH *BURKE*! PREGNANT WITH HIS CHILD AND *STILL* PIRATING OUR SHIPS!

LOOK, RICHARD OF THE IRONS IS *NOTORIOUS* FOR HIS AFFAIRS. AFTER A YEAR AND A DAY THEY'LL SPLIT ...

YOU THINK SHE *CARES*? THIS MARRIAGE IS A SHAM! SHE GIVES HIM A CHILD, HE GIVES HER WESTERN IRELAND!

THEY'LL SPLIT AT A YEAR AND A DAY, PROBABLY FOR THE REASONS YOU SAY ...

... BUT IT'LL BE A *PLAY*, PERFORMED FOR AN AUDIENCE.

WE'LL THINK THEM FRACTURED, AND THAT'S WHEN THEY'LL ATTACK *HARDER*.

WE NEED TO CHANGE OUR ATTACK. WE NEED TO STOP FILLING IRELAND WITH *ENGLISH LORDS*...

... AND CONVERT THE *IRISH* CHIEFTAINS TO OUR SIDE INSTEAD.

THE IRISH SEA.

ENGLISHMEN! I JUST GAVE BIRTH AND I WAS STILL ABLE TO BEAT YOUR COMMANDER!

DO YOU REALLY THINK YOU HAVE A CHANCE AGAINST MY *MEN*? DROP YOUR WEAPONS NOW!

CLATTER

I'M IN A GOOD MOOD RIGHT NOW, SO RETURN TO YOUR SHIP AND BE GONE.

AND TAKE THIS DEAD FOOL WITH YOU.

CAP'N! WHAT IS IT? A BOY OR A GIRL?

A BOY. HIS NAME IS TIBBOT.

BUT I CANNOT ALLOW YOU ENTRY TO THE CASTLE. THE ENGLISH—

CAN BE *DAMNED.* THIS ISN'T ABOUT ME, THOUGH. THIS IS ABOUT THE LAWS OF *HOSPITALITY.*

THIS IS ABOUT YOU REMEMBERING YOUR *HERITAGE.*

FROM NOW ON, YOUR GATES ARE OPEN FOR *ANYONE* WHO NEEDS TO SPEAK TO YOU.

AND EACH NIGHT YOU'LL PUT AN *EXTRA PLACE* AT YOUR TABLE, JUST IN CASE OF UNEXPECTED GUESTS.

NO ONE SHOULD FEEL THE SHAME I DID WHEN TURNED AWAY.

YOU'RE RIGHT, OF COURSE. I AGREE.

NOW RELEASE MY SON—

OH, YOUR SON WAS NEVER A PRISONER. HE FEELS THE SAME WAY I DO. THAT'S WHY HE EATS HIS DINNER IN A *TAVERN.* THOMAS!

THOMAS! I THOUGHT I'D *LOST* YOU!

IF YOU'D KEPT TRYING TO BE LIKE AN *ENGLISH* LORD, FATHER, YOU WOULD HAVE.

ONCE MORE I OWE AN O'MALLEY FOR SAVING MY LIFE, IT SEEMS.

NOTHING MORE THAN A SMALL GUIDING PUSH.

CAP'N! WE GOT *THREE SHIPS* COMING! ENGLISH!

AS PLEASURABLE AS THIS WAS, GENTLEMEN, THE LAST THING I WANT THE ENGLISH TO SEE IS YOU ON MY DECK.

REALLY? I THOUGHT YOU'D BE *HAPPY* TO SEE MORE WAR BETWEEN US!

NO. THERE WILL BE *NO NEGOTIATIONS* WITH THE LIKES OF GRACE O'MALLEY.

YOU CANNOT SPEAK LIKE THAT TO THE *QUEEN!* IT'S TREASON!

NO, IT'S TREASON TO KEEP HER *FROM* THE TRUTH! IRELAND WON'T BOW TO US UNTIL WE *BURN IT TO THE SOIL!*

I'M A SOLDIER. I FIGHT FOR THE CROWN.

I FOUGHT FOR *HENRY.* I FOUGHT FOR *MARY.* I EVEN FOUGHT FOR *LADY JANE* IN THE WEEK OR SO THAT SHE WAS QUEEN.

AND NOW I FIGHT FOR QUEEN ELIZABETH. AND YOU KNOW WHAT I'VE LEARNED IN THOSE YEARS?

THAT KINGS AND QUEENS COME AND GO, BUT DEATH AND THE O'MALLEYS ARE *ALWAYS* THERE.

STOP TRYING TO *COLONISE* THE IRISH. *EXTERMINATE* THEM INSTEAD.

KINGS AND QUEENS MAY COME AND GO, BUT THIS QUEEN STILL *COMMANDS* YOU.

YOU ARE MY SOLDIER? YOU WANT TO FIGHT?

UM, WELL, THAT IS...

THEN YOU CAN FIGHT IN *CYPRUS.*

AND YOU CAN STAY THERE UNTIL YOU LEARN HOW TO *ADDRESS ME IN THE CORRECT MANNER.*

THE IRISH SEA.

GRACE O'MALLEY. THE PIRATE QUEEN, *FINALLY* WHERE SHE BELONGS.

A LUCKY BREAK IN BAD WEATHER, NOTHING MORE. SOON I'LL BE BACK ON THE OCEAN.

WHERE'S MY SON *OWEN*? THEY TOOK HIM FROM ME WHEN WE ARRIVED HERE.

HE TRIED TO ESCAPE. THERE WAS AN ACCIDENT.

YOUR SON IS *DEAD*.

YOU *LIE!*

OH, IT'S ALL TRUE. AND THE FUNNIEST PART OF IT IS THAT WE KNEW WHERE YOU WERE BECAUSE YOUR *OTHER* SON MURROUGH *TOLD* US.

SEEMS HE'S SICK OF BEING IRISH. WANTS TO CHANGE SIDES. GOOD PLAN.

OH, OWEN ... OH, MURROUGH ... WHAT HAVE I DONE TO YOU ...

WELL, I THINK THAT'S *OBVIOUS*. YOU DRAGGED THEM INTO A FUTILE WAR AGAINST A BIGGER OPPONENT.

YOU'RE GOING TO *DIE*, O'MALLEY. YOU'RE GOING TO BE *HANGED* FOR THE TRAITOR YOU ARE. AND THEN WE'LL KILL BURKE AND YOUR OTHER SON.

WHO KNOWS? WE MIGHT EVEN KILL MURROUGH FOR THE *SHEER HELL* OF IT.

FOR **IRELAND!**

THERE. RICHARD'S FIGHTING IN THE VALLEY BELOW.

WE COULD SKIRMISH IN FROM THE SIDE, HELP HIM ON HIS RIGHT FLANK...

IS THAT WHAT I **THINK** IT IS?

THAT'S A **CAVALRY UNIT!** THE ENGLISH MEAN TO CHARGE THE IRISH WHEN IT'S TOO LATE TO RUN!

THEY'LL BE TAKEN BY **SURPRISE!** AND **TRAMPLED!**

THEN LET'S EVEN THE ODDS.

WE'VE PULLED THEM INTO OUR TRAP! SOUND THE HORN!

CALL THE CAVALRY!

WHURP—

WHERE THE HELL ARE THEY? THEY NEED TO — *AH*, HERE THEY ARE.

NO, WAIT. SOMETHING'S NOT *RIGHT* HERE ...

VICTORY!

RICHARD IS DEAD.

YOU NEED TO ELECT A NEW *CHIEFTAIN*. ONE THAT ISN'T TIED TO THE ENGLISH. YOU NEED TO KEEP FIGHTING.

YOU NEED TO COST THE ENGLISH FOR *EVERY YARD OF IRISH LAND* THEY STEAL.

WHAT ABOUT YOU, GRACE O'MALLEY? WE'LL FOLLOW YOU!

I APPRECIATE IT. BUT I HAVE LOST MY *FATHER*, MY *SON*, A *LOVER*, AND *TWO HUSBANDS* TO THE ENGLISH.

YEAH! *PIRATE QUEEN! PIRATE QUEEN!*

I HAVE FOUGHT FOR *DECADES* — FOR NOTHING MORE THAN *BLOOD AND SORROW.*

MY FIGHTING IS *DONE.*

CLARE ISLAND.

IF YOU'VE COME TO *KILL* ME, I BEG YOU — DO IT QUICK.

BECAUSE *NO* SLOW WOUND YOU GIVE ME CAN BETTER THE ONE I GIVE MYSELF.

EVERY DAY I WALK TO THIS SPOT AND WONDER IF I HAVE THE COURAGE TO THROW MYSELF OFF, FACE MY CRIMES IN HEAVEN — OR *HELL*.

WHY, MURROUGH? WHY DID YOU DO IT?

BECAUSE I'M MY FATHER'S SON. BECAUSE I'M AMBITIOUS.

AND BECAUSE I BELIEVED THE ENGLISH *LIES*. THEY SAID YOU'D BOTH BE HELD FOR A FEW MONTHS, NO MORE ...

... THEY SAID THAT NEITHER OF YOU WOULD BE KILLED. THAT WE'D BE LEFT ALONE AFTERWARDS.

AND YET YOUR BROTHER OWEN LIES *DEAD*.

I KNOW! AND *DAMN MY SOUL* FOR HELPING!

THEY *LIED* TO ME! THEY *USED* ME! I'M A *TRAITOR*!

NO, MURROUGH, YOU'RE MY *SON*. AND YOU'LL *ALWAYS* BE AN O'MALLEY.

THIS WASN'T YOUR FAULT. TOGETHER WE'LL FIND THE PERSON *TRULY* RESPONSIBLE.

BUT UNTIL THEN — OUR WAR IS *OVER*.

LATER.

I *DAMN* YOU, BINGHAM. YOU TREACHEROUS SON OF A VIPER.

YOU'RE NOT STILL ANGRY OVER YOUR *BROTHER*, ARE YOU? I TOLD YOU. HE TRIPPED.

ONTO MY DAGGER. *LOTS OF TIMES.*

MURROUGH O'FLAHERTY. OR *O'MALLEY*, WHATEVER YOU CALL YOURSELF THESE DAYS. *DONAL "OF THE PIPES" O'MALLEY* ...

...AND *TIBBOT BURKE*, SON OF THAT TRAITOR RICHARD.

TWO SONS AND A HALF BROTHER. THREE FOR THE PRICE OF ONE.

GOD LOVES ME MORE THAN THE *IRISH* TODAY, IT SEEMS.

THE O'MALLEYS HAVE STOPPED THEIR REBELLION FOR A *YEAR* NOW! WE HAVE NO QUARREL WITH THE ENGLISH!

MY MOTHER, GRACE, HAS NO QUARREL WITH YOU, BINGHAM!

THAT'S A SHAME, BECAUSE I STILL HAVE A QUARREL WITH *HER.*

BURN THE SHIP. TAKE THESE THREE TO THE BRIG. I THINK OUR QUEEN WILL BE *VERY INTERESTED* IN THEM.

CLARE ISLAND.

IT'S FROM ENGLAND. YOUR BROTHER AND YOUR SONS ARE LOCKED IN THE *TOWER OF LONDON*.

RICHARD BINGHAM HAS REQUESTED YOU GIVE YOURSELF UP AND *JOIN* THEM, OR THEY'LL BE EXECUTED.

AND IF I JOIN THEM?

IT DOESN'T SAY.

I FOUGHT FOR IRELAND FOR TWO DECADES, BUT AFTER RICHARD DIED THEY ELECTED AN *ENGLISH PUPPET* AS THE MacWILLIAM, THE HIGH CHIEFTAIN.

I WALKED AWAY FROM BATTLE AND STILL BINGHAM HOUNDS ME.

DAMN MURROUGH! I TOLD HIM *TO LEAVE IT BE!*

HE'S HUNTED FOR BINGHAM ON THE SEAS FOR A YEAR AND HE'S *NEVER* KNOWN WHAT TO DO WHEN HE FOUND HIM!

WHAT MESSAGE SHALL I SEND BACK?

WRITE TO BINGHAM. TELL HIM THAT WE'LL MEET ON THE *OPEN SEAS* TO DISCUSS THIS.

AND THEN I WANT YOU TO WRITE SOME OTHER LETTERS.

ARE YOU *MAD*, GRACE? IT'S A TRAP! HE'LL TURN UP IN THE BIGGEST SHIP HE CAN FIND!

HE'LL *DESTROY* YOU BEFORE YOU EVEN SEE HIM!

OH NO — THIS IS SIR RICHARD BINGHAM.

HE'LL WANT TO LOOK ME IN THE EYE WHEN HE SHOOTS ME.

YOU KNOW IT'S A TRAP AND YOU'RE STILL GOING THROUGH WITH THIS?

WHAT CHOICE DO I HAVE? HE HAS MY KIN.

RAISE THE ANCHOR, BOYS! *IT'S TIME TO SET SAIL!*

BINGHAM IS A SOLDIER, NOT A SAILOR. HE LIKES HIS FIGHTING GROUND TO BE LEVEL, SOLID.

BUT OUT AT SEA, THE WEATHER CAN CHANGE IN THE BLINK OF AN EYE. CALM SEAS BECOME CHOPPY WATERS.

YOU CAN *SINK* AT THE TURN OF A WAVE.

YOU NEED A *STORM* FOR BAD WEATHER! THERE'S NOT A CLOUD IN THE SKY!

I'M AN O'MALLEY. AND MY FATHER TAUGHT ME ...

... O'MALLEYS CREATE STORMS AT WILL.

THE IRISH SEA.

I'M GLAD YOU KEPT TO YOUR SIDE OF THE AGREEMENT, BINGHAM. ONE SHIP, ONE CREW.

NOW I'D LIKE TO DISCUSS THE *OPTIONS* I HAVE TO FREE MY KINSMEN.

THERE ARE NO OPTIONS. YOU'RE UNDER ARREST FOR *TREASON*. YOU AND YOUR WHOLE CREW!

AND HOW ARE YOU GONNA ARREST US, ENGLISHMAN? YOU'RE ONLY ONE SHIP!

YES, I MIGHT HAVE *LIED* ABOUT THAT.

CAPTAIN! *TWO MORE ENGLISH SHIPS* APPROACHING!

YOU *DOUBLE-CROSSED* US! WE CAME HERE IN GOOD FAITH!

YES! AND I'D DO IT A HUNDRED TIMES AGAIN IF IT MEANT THAT I'D STOP YOUR *PIRACY* ON THESE SEAS!

MY ARMADA IS APPROACHING. YOU HAVE NO CHANCE! SURRENDER!

OH, I DON'T THINK SO.

YOU SEE, I THOUGHT THAT YOU'D DO THIS.

MISS GRACE O'MALLEY OF IRELAND.

YOUR MAJESTY, BY THE GRACE OF GOD.

YOU BOW DOWN TO ME? IS THIS HOW QUEENS ARE *SUPPOSED* TO MEET?

I AM NO QUEEN, MA'AM. IT WAS A NICKNAME GIVEN TO ME.

I AM JUST A *MOTHER*, FIGHTING FOR THE LIVES OF HER CHILDREN.

YOUR WORDS DO YOUR EXPLOITS INJUSTICE. THE QUEEN OF PIRATES IS NOT A NICKNAME TO TAKE LIGHTLY.

NOR IS THE FACT THAT YOU CONSTANTLY *DEFY* ME.

I DEFY INVADERS TO MY HOME, YOUR MAJESTY. INVADERS THAT *BURN VILLAGES DOWN* AND *KILL CHILDREN*.

MY APOLOGIES. - SNIFF - IT WAS A COLD JOURNEY AND I FEEL I HAVE CAUGHT A SLIGHT CHILL.

HERE, TAKE MY HANDKERCHIEF.

THANK YOU.

I SAY! *HOW RUDE!*

TO CAST A GIFT AWAY SO CARELESSLY IS AN INSULT. EXPLAIN YOURSELF.

I WAS GIVEN A BEAUTIFUL HANDKERCHIEF, WHICH I THEN *DIRTIED*.

HOW CAN YOU GIVE SOMETHING LIKE THAT *BACK*? HOW CAN YOU KEEP A SULLIED ITEM?

IN IRELAND IT IS CONSIDERED RUDE TO TAKE AN ITEM AND *BREAK* IT. BETTER TO DESTROY IT THAN LIVE WITH THAT SHAME.

I COULDN'T IN GOOD FAITH GIVE YOUR MAID BACK THAT HANDKERCHIEF.

SO HERE, TAKE THIS ONE IN RETURN. MADE FROM THE FINEST MILAN LACE.

OH, UM, THANK YOU.

I... I WASN'T EXPECTING THAT.

OF COURSE NOT, YOUR MAJESTY. YOUR COURTIERS TELL YOU ABOUT A DIFFERENT IRELAND TO THE REAL ONE.

AN IRELAND OF STORY, WHERE WE LIVE IN PIGSTIES AND MARRY GOATS. WHERE WE ARE STUPID, IDIOT PEASANTS ROLLING IN THE MUD.

WHERE WE NEED TO BE RULED BY THE ENGLISH BEFORE WE *KILL OURSELVES*.

THIS IS *YOUR* IRELAND. NOT *MY* IRELAND.

CAPTAIN! *TWO VESSELS APPROACHING!*

ENGLISH SHIPS!

HE'S RIGHT. *DAMN HER!* FOR A MOMENT I BELIEVED IN ELIZABETH'S WORDS!

TWO AGAINST ONE. NOT GOOD ODDS, MA!

NO. THEY'RE NOT.

"THE O'MALLEYS HAVE ALWAYS BEEN ABLE TO CONTROL THE *WEATHER*, GRACE. ONE DAY, YOU'LL KNOW HOW TO DO IT TOO."

DA'! I NEED YOUR HELP *ONE LAST TIME!*

I AM *GRACE O'MALLEY*, AND I CALL FORTH *THUNDER! LIGHTNING!* I CALL A *STORM* LIKE NO OTHER!

LOOKS LIKE THEY CHOSE THE *SECOND* OPTION.

LUCKY FOR US.

I HAVEN'T HAD A CHANCE TO SAY IT YET, BUT *THANK YOU*, MA.

AFTER EVERYTHING I'VE DONE, TO COME AND SAVE ME...

YOU'RE *KIN*, MURROUGH. OF COURSE I'D SAVE YOU.

BESIDES, YOU HAD *TIBBOT* AND YOUR *UNCLE DONAL* ON YOUR SHIP...

...AND I LIKE THEM *MORE* THAN YOU.

MOTHER!

COME ON, LET'S GET HOME.

LET'S ENJOY THE PEACE WHILE IT LASTS.

LONDON.

SIR RICHARD, IT HAS BEEN A **WHILE** SINCE YOU GRACED OUR PRESENCE AT COURT. YOUR INJURY HEALS?

AS WELL AS IT CAN, YOUR MAJESTY. BY THE GRACE OF GOD I LIVE, AND THAT IS ENOUGH FOR ME.

I MUST ADMIT, I DO FIND IT **STRANGE** THAT IMMEDIATELY AFTER **GAINING PARDON** FOR HER FAMILY AND LEAVING COURT ...

... THE FIRST THING SHE DOES IS HUNT YOU DOWN AND **SKEWER** YOU.

NOT QUITE THE ACTIONS OF A WOMAN WHO WANTS **PEACE**, WOULD YOU SAY?

I AGREE, MA'AM. AND THIS IS THE REASON WE MUST **CONTINUE** OUR PURGE OF IRELAND ...

... THEIR PEOPLE **CAN'T BE TRUSTED** TO NEGOTIATE WITH!

I MIGHT NOT AGREE WITH YOUR **METHODS**, SIR RICHARD, BUT YOU DID BRING ME RESULTS.

RETURN TO YOUR DUTIES, BUT WITH A **LIGHTER HAND** THIS TIME.

THEY WON'T EVEN KNOW THAT I'M THERE, YOUR MAJESTY.

"WHAT WOULD YOU DO IF SPAIN INVADED TODAY? ANGLIA TAKEN IN A WEEK? AN INVASION AS VICIOUS AS THE VIKINGS?"

YOUR MAJESTY? ARE YOU ALL RIGHT?

I HAVE SPENT MY **WHOLE LIFE** FACING ENEMIES AT EVERY CORNER.

PEOPLE WHO NEVER WANTED ME AS QUEEN, PEOPLE WHO DON'T WANT ME TO **STAY** AS QUEEN.

MANY OF THEM ARE FAMILY.

ADD TO THEM THE PROBLEMS CURRENTLY WITH **SPAIN**, OUR UNSTABLE ALLIANCES WITH THE **FRENCH** AND THE **DUTCH** ...

... EVEN MY FATHER NEVER FACED WAR FROM SO MANY DIRECTIONS.

I **NEED** IRELAND.

AND SO I MAKE AN ENEMY OF THE **ONE WOMAN** THAT I'VE FELT UNDERSTOOD ME THE BEST.

AT LEAST SHE WAS ABLE TO SAVE HER KIN. THAT'S A SMALL VICTORY.

SIR RICHARD BINGHAM **RETURNS** TO IRELAND.

LIFE GOES ON.

LADY O'MALLEY! LADY O'MALLEY!

NEWS FROM DUBLIN! RICHARD BINGHAM HAS RETURNED!

I DIDN'T THINK THIS PEACE COULD LAST. WHAT ELSE DOES DUBLIN SAY?

THEY SAY THAT HE MEANS TO *DESTROY* O'MALLEY LANDS!

OF *COURSE* HE DOES.

SOME WARS NEVER END.

AND SOME WARS ONLY END IN *BLOOD AND PAIN.*

COME ON, O'MALLEYS...

... IT'S TIME TO *DEFEND OUR LANDS* AGAIN.

THE O'MALLEYS FOUGHT THE ENGLISH AGAIN THROUGHOUT THE NINE YEARS' WAR. GRACE O'MALLEY *NEVER STOPPED* DEFENDING HER HOMELAND.

SHE DIED, AGED *73*, IN 1603, AT HER HOME, SURROUNDED BY HER FAMILY. IT WAS THE SAME YEAR THAT *QUEEN ELIZABETH I* DIED.

TONY LEE

Tony Lee has written for many popular comic books, including *X-Men, Doctor Who, Spider Man, Starship Troopers, Wallace & Gromit,* and *Shrek.* His adaptation of *Pride & Prejudice & Zombies: The Graphic Novel* was a #1 *New York Times* bestseller. He is also the author of the graphic novels *Outlaw: The Legend of Robin Hood, Excalibur: The Legend of King Arthur,* and *Messenger: The Legend of Joan of Arc.* He has also adapted Anthony Horowitz's bestselling series *The Power of Five* into graphic novels. Tony Lee lives in London.

SAM HART

Sam Hart is an illustrator of comic books and graphic novels, including
Judge Dredd and *Starship Troopers*. He is the illustrator of Tony Lee's *Outlaw:
The Legend of Robin Hood*, *Excalibur: The Legend of King Arthur*, and *Messenger:
The Legend of Joan of Arc*. Sam Hart lives and teaches comic art in Brazil.